Harmonica Course

The absolute beginner's guide to playing harmonica in full color!

INCLUDES
DVD
Video Instruction
CD
With Demos and Backing Tracks

AMSCO PUBLICATIONS
London/New York/Paris/Sydney/Copenhagen/Madrid

FREE ONLINE SUPPORT

Exclusive Distributors:
Music Sales Corporation
257 Park Avenue South
New York
NY 10010, USA.

Music Sales Limited
8/9 Frith Street,
London W1D 3JB, England.

Music Sales Pty Limited
120 Rothschild Avenue,
Rosebery, NSW 2018,
Australia.

Order No. AM989648
ISBN-10: 0-8256-3549-7
ISBN-13: 978-0-8256-3549-6

Written by Steve Jennings.
Photographs by George Taylor and Gary Franco.
Book design by Chloë Alexander.

Printed in China

Contents

Introduction

Welcome to *icanplaymusic Harmonica*.
The harmonica is one of the most popular instruments in the world—this book will guide you from the very first time you pick up your harmonica right through to playing some of the world's best-loved melodies.

Easy-to-follow instructions
will guide you through:

- reading harmonica notation
- playing chords and single notes
- playing your first song

Play along with the backing track as you learn—the specially recorded CD will let you hear how the music *should* sound—then try playing the part yourself.

Practice regularly and often. Twenty minutes every day is far better than two hours on the weekend with nothing in between. Not only are you training your brain to understand how to play the harmonica, you are also teaching your muscles to memorize certain repeated actions.

What sort of harmonica do I need?

For this book you'll need what is known as a 10-hole Richter-tuned major diatonic harmonica in the key of C (phew!). Most players refer to this as the *C Harp*.

If you are concerned you are not getting the right harmonica, just make sure it has 10 holes and is marked with the letter "C."

10-hole major diatonic harmonica

How do harmonicas work?

Diatonic means that your harmonica can play the standard seven notes: do, re, me, fa, sol, la, ti (do— we don't count the last note, since it is the same as the first, only higher…).

The diatonic harmonica has two reeds for each of its ten holes. The harmonica is a *free reed* instrument, because the tone it creates is the sound of the reeds vibrating freely, rather than against the plate to which they are attached. In effect, the reeds are like valves, which open and close to allow air to pass through the chamber created by your mouth and the harmonica itself. What you hear is the vibration of the air, caused by the movement of the reeds, resonating in your mouth.

When you *blow* into the harmonica, the top reeds open and the bottom reeds close into their channels. When you *draw* (the harmonica player's term for sucking air through the instrument), the bottom reeds open up and the top reeds close.

So here's the bad news: if you want to sound like Dylan, Sonny Boy, or one of the other harmonica greats, it simply isn't going to happen, at least not exactly. This is because the sound the harmonica makes when you play is unique to you—the way you breathe, the shape of your mouth and other indefinable characteristics all affect the ultimate sound.

Getting a sound

Playing the harmonica is easy! To demonstrate this, let's do what you have probably done already: pick up your harmonica, making sure that the numbers over the holes are on top, place your lips over the first three holes, and blow gently. If your harmonica doesn't have numbered holes, you'll have to blow into it to see which end has the low notes and which end has the high notes. The low notes go to your left.

You have just played a C chord! If you do the same thing again but this time *draw* air gently through the harmonica, you'll get a G chord. Easy, huh?

So, now we've warmed up, turn the page to start learning even more…

Getting Started

Here are a few simple points about music and how it's written:

Music is notated on five equally spaced lines called a *staff*:

The squiggly thing at the beginning of the staff is known as a *treble clef*. There are other clefs, but for our purposes this is the only one you need to know. The position of notes on the lines and spaces of the staff, or above and below it, shows you their *pitch*.

All musical sounds or notes have pitches—how low or how high they happen to be. The notes also have names taken from the first seven letters of the alphabet:

A   B   C   D   E   F   G

After G, we start again at A. This is because although the second A is "higher" than the first one, they sound very similar, and also because if each individual pitch had a unique name you'd need to have a memory like a computer to retain them all—whereas the alphabet you already know!

The staff is divided into *measures* by the use of vertical barlines:

barline   double
                                           barline

6

Each measure has a fixed number of *beats* in it. A beat is the natural tapping rhythm of a song—when you tap your foot to a piece of music you're responding to the beat. Most tunes have four beats in a measure, so you would count and/or tap your foot like this:

The two 4s set one above the other in the example above are what is called a *time signature*. The top number tells you how many beats there are in each measure—you don't need to worry about the bottom number for the time being.

As well as pitch, notes have *duration*—they last for a certain length of time. We'll introduce the different note durations as we go along. The first note we're going to use is the *whole note*, which looks like this:

A whole note lasts for four beats. Each type of note length has an equivalent *rest* to indicate that you remain silent for the same number of beats. A whole-rest looks like this:

CHECKPOINT

WHAT YOU'VE ACHIEVED SO FAR...

You can now:
• Understand basic concepts of pitch, rhythm and counting

Holding Your Harmonica

Hold your harmonica between the thumb and forefinger of your left hand, with the soundholes facing you and the numbers on top, like this:

Now place your right hand like this:

If you are left handed, simply carry out these steps starting with your right hand.

Your "cupping" hand that wraps around the back is used to control the volume of the sound you produce. Using the thumb as a pivot, move the hand away and toward you while blowing and listen to the difference in sound. When this is done quickly, it is what is known as a "wah-wah" and is heard a lot in harmonica music. For the time being, leave your hand cupped around the back as shown in the photographs.

Tip

You may find it helps to imagine the sound you are producing as like a ping-pong ball supported on the column of air coming from your lungs, and if you blow too hard the ball will fall (but it won't break—stay relaxed!).

Blow for Four

The first piece is titled "Blow for Four," because that's all you need to do—simply blow for four beats, then rest for four beats. Use any combination of blow notes anywhere on the harmonica or practice the C chord you learned earlier, but remember not to play during the rests—it will sound awful if you do! The whole notes are only there to show you when to play—you choose which holes to use.

Don't forget to count, as indicated, and notice that at the end you play two *chords* (as two or more notes sounded together are called) in successive measures. Listen to **Track 1** to hear how it sounds. You will hear the drummer tapping the time for two measures before the band comes in—this is so that you know how fast your own counting should be.

Now try it yourself with **Track 2**.

Count: 1   2   3   4 | 1   2   3   4 | 1   2   3   4 | 1   2   3   4

1   2   3   4 | 1   2   3   4 | 1   2   3   4 | 1   2   3   4

Harmonica maintenance

The reeds themselves are particularly delicate and it is important to keep them clean and correctly positioned. There is no getting around the fact that playing the harmonica can be a messy business, especially when your band is really rocking, so it is essential to tap the extraneous material out of your harmonica before you put it away.

If you find that some notes are not working properly you can, with care, gently lift off the top and bottom plates of the harmonica to reveal the reed plates within. Carefully check that the reeds are sitting neatly in their slots and that they are clean, with no blockages to prevent them from opening and shutting smoothly. If necessary, you can clean them with a damp cotton swap, but be careful to ensure you leave no threads behind.

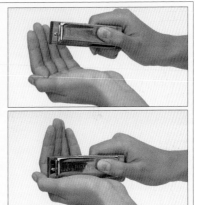

Finding Notes

Now let's pick out some specific notes on your instrument.

To do this you need to know:
1 What specific notes look like in written music, and
2 What they look like in special harmonica tablature.

Bear in mind that while harmonica tablature is a way of making music-reading easier for you, it is not a substitute for reading music.

Locate hole 5 on your harmonica, either by using the tip of your tongue to count up from hole 1, or by hand/eye coordination.

When you've "hit the spot," take your tongue away and blow hole 5 together with the two adjacent holes (4 and 6).

Listen carefully to **Track 3** and make sure that you're getting the same sound from your harmonica.

Notice that the hole numbers you need to play are stacked one above the other, like the musical notes they correspond to, and that in this example you see three plain numbers.

Plain numbers mean: blow that hole or combination of holes.

Next, try drawing, or sucking on, the same holes.

Remember that you should not be using force. Just breathe in gently through your mouth—the reeds on the harmonica know what their purpose is, and they will respond to very little air pressure. Again, listen carefully to **Track 4** and check that you're getting the same chord from your harmonica.

Notice that this time the numbers have circles around them and—you guessed it—circles mean draw on that hole or combination of holes.

The written music looks like this:

With the TAB (tablature) it looks like this:

The written music looks like this:

And with the TAB:

Blow for Four, Draw for More

When you're sure that you're matching the sounds I'm making on the CD, play this little piece, which is a development of "Blow for Four," entitled

"Blow for Four, Draw for More." Listen to **Track 5** and then play along with **Track 6**.

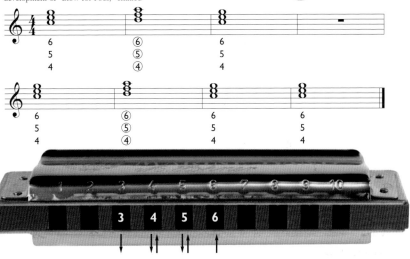

When you're happy with this, try moving from **blowing** ↑ 4, **5**, and **6** to **drawing** ↓ 3, 4, and **5**.

Use the tip of your tongue, as before, to locate hole 4. Don't take the instrument out of your mouth—you need to learn to sense where you are on the harp without looking. Make sure that your mouth shape does not change, and move the instrument, not your head.

Once you are confident that you can change from 4, 5 and 6 to 3, 4 and 5 with ease, try this, a practice version of a song coming up on page 13. **Track 7** demonstrates how this should sound.

Track 8 gives you just the backing track without the recorded harmonica. Remember to count for two measures with the "click" before starting.

Harmonica Notation

You will have noticed by now that each note on the staff corresponds to a number in the tablature. The following diagrams will enable you to see what the name of each note is, where it is on the harmonica, and what it looks like written in music and tablature:

Track 11 demonstrates how it sounds.

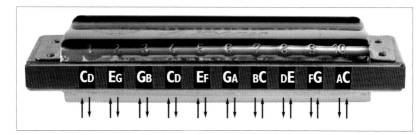

Before we move on, here's some more information about musical notation.

The whole note can be divided into two, which produces two notes called *half notes*, each of which is two beats in length.
Here they are with their rest:

Now try the full version of "Goin' Around." Listen to **Track 9** to hear how it sounds, then play along with **Track 10**. Don't forget to count!

Another Rhythm

Logically enough, half notes can also be divided in half, giving us two *quarter notes,* each of which lasts for one beat. Here they are with their rest:

Count: 1   2   3   4   1   2   3   4

Jingle Bells

"Jingle Bells" uses some new note combinations as well as all the note values you have learned so far.

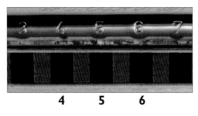

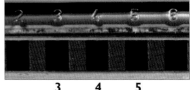

To separate the notes, we're going to use a technique called *tonguing.* As you start each note, move your tongue as if you were saying "dah." You will find that this gives a sharper sound to the note than if you begin it in your throat.

Listen to **Track 12** to hear how "Jingle Bells" should sound, and then try it yourself with **Track 13**.

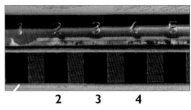

CHECKPOINT

WHAT YOU'VE ACHIEVED SO FAR...

You can now:
- Read specific notes from musical notation and harmonica tablature
- Tell from tablature whether to draw or blow
- Play three-note chords

Jingle Bells

Traditional

Jin - gle	bells,		jin - gle	bells,		jin - gle	all	the	way.
5	5	5	5	5	5	5	6	4	④	5
4	4	4	4	4	4	4	5	3	③	4
3	3	3	3	3	3	3	4	2	②	3

Oh	what	fun	it	is	to	ride	a	one - horse	o - pen	sleigh.	Hey!
⑤	⑤	⑤	⑤	⑤	5	5	5	5	④	④	5	④	6
④	④	④	④	④	4	4	4	4	③	③	4	③	5
③	③	③	③	③	3	3	3	3	②	②	3	②	4

Jin - gle	bells,		jin - gle	bells,		jin - gle	all	the	way.
5	5	5	5	5	5	5	6	4	④	5
4	4	4	4	4	4	4	5	3	③	4
3	3	3	3	3	3	3	4	2	②	3

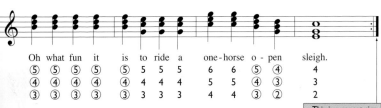

Oh	what	fun	it	is	to	ride	a	one - horse	o - pen	sleigh.
⑤	⑤	⑤	⑤	⑤	5	5	5	6	6	⑤	④	4
④	④	④	④	④	4	4	4	5	5	④	③	3
③	③	③	③	③	3	3	3	4	4	③	②	2

This is a repeat sign.
When you see this, go
back to the beginning
or to 𝄆 and play again.

15

Two Notes Only

Now it's time to try to play only two holes at a time, rather than the three you've been using so far. This is a little bit more tricky, as you're going to have to be more precise.

The easiest way of doing this is to feel with the tip of your tongue for the little upright post between the two holes so as to line it up with the center of your mouth, then play those holes. Obviously, you should put your tongue away again once you've located the correct position!

Skip to My Lou

In "Skip to My Lou" you should try to separate the eighth notes using a technique called "double-tonguing." Happily, this does not mean that you have to acquire another tongue from somewhere. Double-tonguing simply means that for the first eighth note in a pair you move your tongue as if you were saying "dah," and for the second eighth note you move your tongue as if you were saying "k" (as in "kite").

Listen to **Track 14**, "Skip to My Lou," and try to follow the score while you listen.

Now try playing along yourself with **Track 15**.

The next piece also introduces a new note value, the *eighth note*. These last for half a beat and are counted like this:

Like all the other note values you've come across, the eighth note has an equivalent rest, which looks like this:

> ## Tip
>
> When more than one eighth note occurs in a row, they are joined up with a *beam*. This doesn't make any difference to the rhythm of the music—it just makes it easier to read.

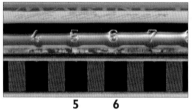

5   6

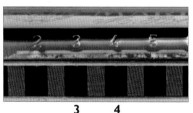

3   4

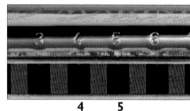

4   5

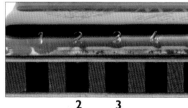

2   3

Skip to My Lou

Traditional

Lost my part-ner, skip to my Lou, lost my part-ner, skip to my Lou,

5 5 4 4 5 5 5 6 ④ ④ ③ ③ ④ ④ ④ ⑤
4 4 3 3 4 4 4 5 ③ ③ ② ② ③ ③ ③ ④

lost my part-ner, skip to my Lou, skip to my Lou my dar - lin'.

5 5 4 4 5 5 5 6 ④ 5 ⑤ 5 ④ 4 4
4 4 3 3 4 4 4 5 ③ 4 ④ 4 ③ 3 3

Lou, Lou, skip to my Lou, Lou, Lou, skip to my Lou,

5 4 5 5 5 6 ④ ③ ④ ④ ④ ⑤
4 3 4 4 4 5 ③ ② ③ ③ ③ ④

Lou, Lou, skip to my Lou, skip to my Lou my dar - lin'.

5 4 5 5 5 6 ④ 5 ⑤ 5 ④ 4 4
4 3 4 4 4 5 ③ 4 ④ 4 ③ 3 3

17

Dotted Notes

The next piece introduces a new note value, the *sixteenth note,* which looks like an eighth note, but with two little tails instead of one. As you've probably guessed, a sixteenth note lasts for a quarter of a beat and is counted like this:

Just like all the other note values, a sixteenth note has an equivalent rest, which looks like this:

One last point about note values. Any note can have a "dot" added to it which increases its value by half. Thus a dotted whole note is six beats, a dotted half note equals three beats, a dotted quarter note equals one and a half beats, and so on.

Tip

Like the eighth note, groups of sixteenth notes can be joined together—this time with a double beam. This doesn't affect their duration—it just makes the music easier to read by grouping together notes that belong to the same beat (or beats).

One very common dotted grouping (which you will see in the next tune) is the dotted eighth note followed by a single sixteenth note. It looks and is counted like this:

The dotted eighth note equals three sixteenth notes, and the single sixteenth note at the end rounds out each beat.

Brown Girl in the Ring

This is the last tune you will play using two-note chords—listen to **Track 16** and then try it yourself with **Track 17.**

If you have trouble with the faster passages, isolate them and practice them slowly until you can play each pair of notes cleanly. Once you can do that at a slower speed, gradually increase the tempo until you can play along with the audio.

Tip

Use double-tonguing for the groups of sixteenth notes.

Brown Girl in the Ring

Traditional

Brown	girl	in	the	ring,	tra	- la - la - la - la,
5	5	5	④	4	5	④ 5 ⑤ 6
4	4	4	③	3	4	③ 4 ④ 5

brown	girl	in	the	ring,	tra	- la - la - la - la.	Brown	girl	in	the	ring,
④	④	④	4	③	6	⑥ 6 ⑤ 5 ④	5	5	5	④	4
③	③	③	3	②	5	⑤ 5 ④ 4 ③	4	4	4	③	3

(Play 3 times)

tra	- la - la - la - la,	she	likes	su -	gar,	I	like	plum,	plum,	plum!
5	④ 5 ⑤ 6	7	6	5	5	④	④	4	7	7
4	③ 4 ④ 5	6	5	4	4	③	③	3	6	6

CHECKPOINT

WHAT YOU'VE ACHIEVED SO FAR...

You can now:
* Read eighth notes and sixteeth notes
* Use double-tonguing
* Play two-note chords

19

Playing Single Notes

There are several methods of producing one note at a time from the harmonica. We're going to use the *puckering* or *whistle* method. As the name implies, you pucker your lips as if to whistle, making the hole between your lips about the same size as one of those on the instrument. Or you could try imagining that you're drinking a thick milkshake through a straw.

1 Tighten the muscles at the corner of your lips, since the natural lip position is wider and more disposed to sounding full chords—your upper lip should curl up very slightly toward your nose.

2 Put your upper lip well over the cover of the harp, and your lower lip well under it. The wet inner part of your lips should be in contact with the harmonica, not the dry outer part. This will help to get a good air seal around the hole, reducing any air loss and promoting not only good tone, but also economical breathing.

3 Blow and draw gently on hole 1. You should find this relatively easy, as there is no number 0 hole to interfere with your efforts!

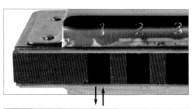

Tip

Remember: the less air you can use, the better— and the longer your harmonica will last!

If you're not sure that you're getting it right, use both your index fingers to cover all the holes except the one you're trying to play. Now play both notes in that hole and try to remember how they sound. Go back to your normal holding position and try to reproduce the sound you made while your fingers were covering the neighboring holes.

Tip

Always remember to move the harmonica across your mouth—don't move your head—it's far less accurate. If you think you're having trouble with this, try practicing in front of a mirror.

Stay relaxed and let your breathing be deep, free and easy. When you're happy that you're able to produce single notes clearly, without interference from neighboring holes and without what is best described as "fuzziness," run through the previous tunes again, but this time play only the top note of each chord shown in the first line of the tablature.

4 Next try hole 4, both blow and draw. Make sure that you are sounding one note and one note only in each breath direction.

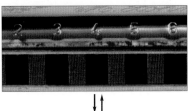

5 Experiment with all the holes on the instrument, making sure that each note sounds clearly. Be careful with the draw notes in holes 2 and 3—it is not uncommon for new harp players to have problems with these. Draw 2 should sound the same as blow 3.

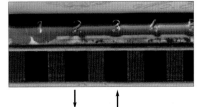

When the Saints Go Marching In

Now let's play a piece of classic jazz. The first measure of "When the Saints Go Marching In" has only three beats—this is known as a *pick-up measure*, and means that the tune starts before the first complete measure. Listen carefully to **Track 18** to see what I mean.

The other thing you haven't encountered before in the music is a *tie*. This is an arc-shaped line that joins two notes of the same pitch—it means play the first note but sustain it for the length of time indicated by the tied notes.

So, for example, the note G (blow 6) that belongs with the word "saints" at the beginning of the tune is played for 1 whole note + 1 quarter note = 5 beats.

Listen to **Track 19** to hear how it sounds, and then try playing along with **Track 20**.

Traditional

Down by the Sally Gardens

Here's a lovely Irish melody—make sure you are playing single notes correctly. To hear the melody listen to **Track 21**.

Watch out for the things which look like ties, except they join notes of different pitches. These marks are known as *slurs* and indicate that the notes they join should run into one another, in much the same way as the words in slurred speech. The slurred notes belong to one syllable of the word, so it can help to "sing" the words in your head as you play the tune in order to get these phrases right.

You can take advantage of the way the harmonica is laid out when playing some of these slurs. Where the slur covers two notes with the same breath direction in neighboring holes, only tongue the first note of the pair, and move the harp while maintaining the airflow. The slur will happen almost automatically. Similarly, if the slur involves a change of breath direction, you will get a smoother effect if you only tongue the first note of the pair. Try it!

Now play along with **Track 22**.

Traditional

The Streets of Laredo

You've now covered the basics of the harmonica—you can play single notes and read harmonica notation and tablature. Now it's time to put your new skills to the test—on the following pages you'll find some popular songs arranged for the harmonica, which will develop your playing even further!

The next tune, that you can find on **Track 23**, sounds great on the harmonica! It has a time-signature of 3/4, otherwise known as waltz time. This means there are only three beats in each measure, rather than the four you're used to—so remember to count 1, 2, 3 / 1, 2, 3 and so on. Try playing along with **Track 24**.

Traditional

As I walked out in the streets of La-
6 6 ⑤ 5 ⑤ 6 ⑤ 5 ④ 4

-re-do, as I walked out in La-
③ 3 3 4 4 ④ 5 ⑤

-re-do one day, I spied a poor
5 ④ 4 ④ 6 6 ⑤ 5

cow-boy all wrapped in white li-nen, all
⑤ 6 ⑤ 5 ④ 4 ③ 3 3

(Play 3 times)

wrapped in white li-nen as cold as the day.
4 ③ 4 ④ 5 ⑤ 5 ③ ④ 4

Annie Laurie

This is a well-known Scottish melody. Watch out for the big jumps from hole 4 to hole 7, and make sure that you are playing them accurately. If necessary, isolate that jump and practice it slowly. Listen to **Track 25**, then try playing along with **Track 26**.

The tune also makes use of the high register of the harmonica. You will need to keep your throat very open to prevent these notes from sounding squeaky, and bear in mind that they require a little less breath and a little more control to get them to sound sweet.

Traditional

| Max | Well - ton | braes | are | bon - nie | where | ear - ly | falls | the— |
| 4 | 4 | 4 | 7 | 7 | ⑦ ⑥ | ⑥ | 6 | 5 5 ④ 4 |

dew.— And it's there that An - nie Lau - rie gave
5 ④ 5 ④ 4 4 7 7 ⑦ ⑥ ⑥

me her pro - mise true, gave me her pro - mise true, which
6 5 5 ④ 4 6 7 7 ⑧ ⑧ 8 6

ne'er for - got will be. And for bon - nie bon - nie An - nie
7 7 ⑧ ⑧ 8 8 ⑧ 7 ⑦ ⑥ ⑦ 7 ⑥

(Play 3 times)

Lau - rie I'd— lay— me doon and dee.
6 5 5 ④ 4 7 5 5 ④ 4

25

My Bonnie Lies over the Ocean

This old favorite again uses the high notes of the harmonica, and is also in waltz time.

Listen to **Track 27**, and play along with **Track 28**.

Traditional

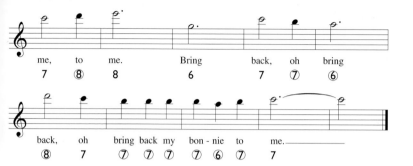

me,   to   me.   Bring   back,   oh   bring
7   ⑧   8   6   7   ⑦   ⑥

back,   oh   bring back my bon - nie   to   me.
⑧   7   ⑦ ⑦ ⑦ ⑦ ⑥ ⑦   7

CHECKPOINT

WHAT YOU'VE ACHIEVED SO FAR...

You can now:
- Play two-note chords
- Read eighth-note rhythms
- Understand dotted notes
- Play single notes
- Give a concert to family and friends playing all the tunes you've learned!

Twinkle, Twinkle, Little Star

Try to play this gently and quietly. One of the best ways of putting music across is to hold a strong image in your mind of what it is that you are trying to convey. If you can see it, your listeners will too; so with this tune try to imagine the sense of wonder that a child has as he or she looks up at the stars through the night sky. This children's favorite introduces a new time signature, 2/4. There are only two beats in each measure, so count **1**, **2 – 1**, **2** etc.

Listen to **Track 29** and play along with **Track 30**.

Traditional

O Christmas Tree

Track 31 is an arrangement of this well-known carol in 3/4 time—pay particular attention to the dotted eighth note/sixteenth note pairs.

Track 32 provides the accompaniment for you to play along with.

Traditional

O Christ - mas Tree, O Christ - mas Tree, you stand in ver - dant
3   4   4   4   ④   5   5   5   ④   5   ⑤   ③

beau - ty! O Christ - mas Tree, O Christ - mas Tree, you
④   4   3   4   4   4   ④   5   5   5   5

stand in ver - dant beau - ty! Your boughs are green in
④   5   ⑤   ③   ④   4   6   6   5   ⑥   6

sum - mer's glow and do not fade in win - ter's snow. O
6   ⑤   ⑤   ⑤   ⑤   ④   6   ⑤   ⑤   5   5   3

(Play 3 times)

Christ - mas Tree, O Christ - mas Tree, you stand in ver - dant beau - ty!
4   4   4   ④   5   5   5   5   ④   5   ⑤   ③   ④   4

Carrickfergus

This arrangement of the traditional Irish melody is also in 3/4 time. Watch out for the slurs here, and try to play them as smoothly as possible.
Listen to **Track 33**.

The backing track is on **Track 34**.

Traditional

-grand._____ But the sea is wide_____
4   6   6   6   6   7

_____ and I can-not swim o - ver,
        7 ⑧ 8 ⑧ 7 ⑧ ⑦   6

and nei - ther have_____   I__
6   6   6   7   ⑧ 8

wings to fly._____   I wish I
⑨   8   ⑧   7   7   ⑦

had_____   a hand - some
⑥   ④   5   ⑤   6

boat - man_____   to fer - ry me
5   ④   4   4   ④   ④   5

o - ver_____   my love__ and I.
⑤ 5 ④   ③   4   ④   4

The Bluebells of Scotland

This should not present you with too many difficulties. **Track 35** is the demonstration track.

Track 36 is the backing track.

Traditional

O where, tell me where is your— high-land lad-die
6   7   ⑦   ⑥   6   ⑥   ⑦   7   5   5   ⑤   ④

gone?   O   where,   tell   me   where   is   your—
4   6   7   ⑦   ⑥   6   ⑥   ⑦   7

high-land lad-die   gone?   He's   gone   with   stream-ing
5   5   ⑤   ④   4   6   5   4   5   6

ban - ners,   where   no - ble   deeds   are   done.   And   it's
7   ⑥   7   ⑦   6   ⑥   6   6   ⑥   ⑦

oh!   In   my   heart,   I———   wish   him   safe   at   home.
7   ⑦   ⑥   6   ⑥   ⑦   7   5   5   ⑤   ④   4

The Yellow Rose of Texas

The remaining tunes will expand your repertoire without introducing any new techniques or note values.

Listen to **Track 37** for the demo and play along with **Track 38**.

Traditional

There's a	yel - low	rose	in	Tex - as	I'm	go - ing	home	to
6 ⑤	5 6	6	6	⑥ 6	⑤	5 6	7	⑧

see,	she	wants	no	oth - er	fel - low,	no -
8	6	6	8	8 8	8 ⑧	7

bo - dy,	on - ly	me.	Oh, she	cried	so	when	I
⑦ 7	⑧ 8	⑧	6 ⑤	5	6	6	6

left	her	that	it	near - ly	broke	my	heart,	and	I
⑥	6	6	⑤	5 6	7	⑧	8	6	6

(Play 3 times)

hope	that	when	we	meet	a - gain	we	nev - er - more	will	part.
6	⑨	⑨	⑨	⑨	8 ⑧	7	7 6	8 ⑧	7

The Leaving of Liverpool

Track 39 is the demo track.

Track 40 is the backing track.

Traditional

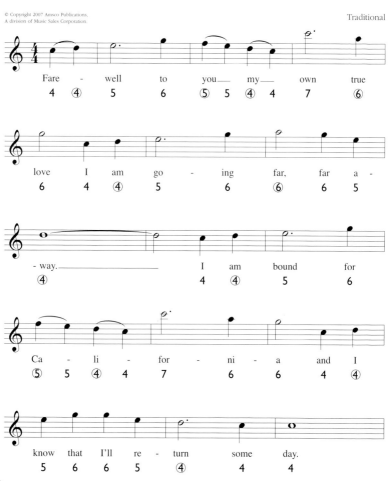

Fare	-	well	to	you—	my—	own	true
4	④	5	6	⑤ 5	④ 4	7	⑥

love	I	am	go	-	ing	far,	far	a -
6	4	④	5		6	⑥	6	5

- way.—		I	am	bound	for
④		4	④	5	6

Ca	-	li	-	for	-	ni	-	a	and	I
⑤	5	④	4	7		6		6	4	④

know	that	I'll	re	-	turn	some	day.
5	6	6	5		④	4	4

34

So fare thee well my love, my ———
7 ⑦ 7 ⑧ ⑦ 6 ⑦ ⑧

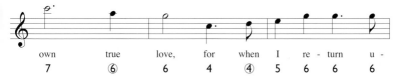

own true love, for when I re - turn u -
7 ⑥ 6 4 ④ 5 6 6 6

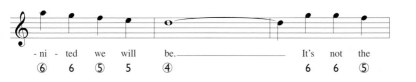

- ni - ted we will be. ——————— It's not the
⑥ 6 ⑤ 5 ④ 6 6 ⑤

leav - ing of Liv - er - pool that grieves —— me, but my
5 5 6 ⑤ 5 ④ 4 7 ⑥ 6 4 ④

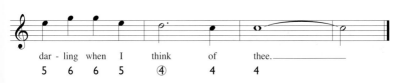

dar - ling when I think of thee. ——————
5 6 6 5 ④ 4 4

Putting on the Style

There are all kinds of little tricks and devices available to you to add expression to your playing. I have attempted to describe some of the simpler techniques here but, as always, trial and error will probably introduce you to many more, including some that may be unique to you.

Tongued notes

To add attack, or to create a staccato effect, go "dah" with the tip of your tongue against the roof of your mouth. It's as if you are playing the tune as you might sing a song when you don't know the words: "dah-de-dah-de-dah-de-dah," and so on. Indeed, as you experiment with your playing, you will find that most of these tricks and effects are created by making vocal-like shapes and noises; this is what makes the harmonica so expressive as an instrument.

> This is a basic technique, which gives extra clarity and emphasis to each note or chord. Use it freely between the smooth draws and blows to create contrast and extra rhythmic punch.

The "Wah"

A staple for blues harmonica players, the "wah" involves the use of the hands as well as the mouth. Hold the harmonica in the way shown at the start of the book (with your hand cupped around the back). Then, as you blow and draw, open and close your hand.

> Vary the speed to gain different effects, from a fast tremolo to a haunting cry.

Trills

This is the other essential blues effect—the sound of two alternate notes played rapidly. Once you have mastered single notes, this is just a matter of hand control. Draw or blow a note, then move the harmonica (NOT your head) from side to side between your original note and the one above or below it. Try doing it slowly first—the draw notes on holes 4 and 5 are good places to start. Make sure you are getting good, clean notes on each hole before you try going faster; the effect is spoiled if you have too much blurring.

> The trill increases intensity in a song—try it on a long note and you'll see what I mean.

Tremolo

This is a rapid variation in the volume of a note. This style is a little tricky and may take some practice. To achieve this style you have to be breathing properly from your diaphragm. You have to choke your breath intermittently right at the back of your throat and down into your windpipe. Really, you should focus on your stomach. Try going "UH-UH-UH-UH" with your voice deep in your throat and you'll get some idea of how it's done, but don't allow the effect to come from your throat. You've got to go way down further.

> Listen to Sonny Boy Williamson's "Mighty Long Time" for the finest demonstration of this effect and note how vocal the playing is. He is virtually sobbing into the harmonica, which is effectively what you have to do. That's why they call it the blues...

Vibrato

This is a rapid variation in pitch, much used by opera singers to add color to the high notes. You can achieve a similar effect on the harmonica by moving the middle of your tongue up and down quickly. You can pair this up with a fast "wah" to add extra wobble.

> Don't over do this! Vibrato is great to emphasize a point, not to color a whole song.

Tongue trills

A richer type of trill, this is simply a question of drawing or blowing several notes at once (a chord) and flicking your tongue from side to side across the holes.

> Try drawing or blowing the chord without the trill first, then use your tongue to add that extra dimension of color. Also, vary the speed of the flicking to achieve different kinds of emotional impact.

Fast trills and rasps

John Lennon used this technique in his harmonica playing on "Love Me Do." You simply allow the air to vibrate the side or tip of your tongue rapidly against the roof of your mouth, creating a machine gun-like effect.

> Definitely not one to be over-used—this is not a "pretty" effect, but it has occasional novelty value.

The train

This is one of the best-loved effects and one that is fundamental to the playing of Sonny Terry and his emulators in particular. It's easy once you have control of your tongue. Try going "dugga-dugga-dugga" as you draw on the low notes and you will soon get the hang of it. Notice that the tip and back of your tongue are touching the roof of your mouth in quick-fire succession.

> Try moving your lips backwards and forwards as you chug, and notice the change in tone, reflecting the sound of the engine as it carried the promise of a better life—or the sound of a departing lover—to the workers in the cotton fields...

Congratulations!

I hope that you've enjoyed playing through this book and that you will feel inspired to carry on making music on your harmonica in whichever style most interests you. Feel free to ask other players about their experience and techniques, and remember to have fun. Making music should be an enjoyable experience!

To hear how the pros do it, check out some recordings by these influential harmonica players:

Jerry Portnoy (Muddy Waters, Eric Clapton)
Lee Oskar
Charlie Musselwaite (John Lee Hooker)
Paul Butterfield (The Butterfield Blues Band)
Brendan Power (Riverdance)
Norton Buffalo (The Steve Miller Band)

Harmonica Classics

Now that you've grasped the fundamentals of harmonica playing, try listening to how the professionals do it! The songs listed to the right all feature classic harmonica parts; some are more difficult than others, but armed with the basic techniques you've learned in this book, you should soon be able to approach some of them.

Good Morning Little School Girl John Mayall
Love Me Do The Beatles
Magic Bus The Who
Midnight Rambler Rolling Stones
Mr. Tambourine Man Bob Dylan
The River Bruce Springsteen
There Must Be an Angel Eurythmics (Stevie Wonder)
Heart of Gold Neil Young

Bob Dylan

Neil Young

Bruce Springsteen

www.LearnAsYouPlay.com

Turn your playing up a notch with the click of a mouse!

Visit http://www.learnasyouplay.com
for free additional instructional materials
including professional tips,
supplemental music materials, and more!

Build upon the skills you've already mastered
and watch your playing improve substantially.